CAN'T BURY TALES

short stories inside a short story

CATHY SPROUL

21st Century Renaissance Press

21st Century Renaissance Press

Manufactured in the United States of America

Cover Design by Bighorn Termite/shutterstock

ISBN-13: 978-0692259054
ISBN: 0692259058

For my parents

CONTENTS

Though try they may to render it confined,
restrictions cannot help but spur the mind.

THE GENERAL PROLOGUE

When in November rain sells out to snow
and Zephyr's heading south to Mexico,
the yellows, reds, and oranges fade to brown
and rot like little corpses on the ground.
A stark sobriety impairs the grass,
the sting of Scorpio has come to pass,
and those who speak of April sound like liars.

At any rate, a pilgrimage transpires,
and all the rats who scratch and claw their way
to dumpy offices and back each day
instead embark on journeys to appease

their preciously annoying families,
inhale their turkey dinners, drink their booze,
and watch their favorite football franchise lose.

But who was I to judge? A rat as well.
As such, I packed my bags and drove like hell,
arriving at the airport none too soon
that madhouse of a Wednesday afternoon
and flew across the country to O'Hare—
but didn't land. There was a blizzard there.

We circled in the air, the windows clouded.
The pilot soon announced, "We've been rerouted.
I'm sorry, but the storm's beyond our power.
We're landing in Detroit in half an hour."

Disgusted, I reacted to the news
by bitching, "Isn't there a ground crew who's
supposed to be dispersing runway salt?"
The flight attendant said, "It's no one's fault,"
and glared at me. I chose not to pursue
it. Either way, the situation blew.

We landed, taxied through the slushy muck,
and disembarked—into a clusterfuck
of magnitude that dwarfed my wildest dreams.
The terminal was bursting at the seams.
I hiked to baggage claim—a major feat—
and failed to spot a single empty seat.
There was no chance to score an SUV:
the rental lines stretched on eternally.

For such a seasoned traveler, you know,
I couldn't think of anywhere to go.

So I stood with a group of others who
had no idea what the hell to do.
We hung out by the automatic doors,
which led to cabs and limos and, of course,
the shuttle busses heading to downtown
and other transportation on the ground.

Then — out of nowhere — from the curb outside
this guy appeared and offered us a ride.
The dude was short and bald. His name was Fred —
at least that's what his plastic nametag said.
His bulging gut looked like a pregnancy
and, truth be told, he didn't seem to be
the brightest lightning bug, the slyest fox,
or sharpest hook inside the tackle box —
you get the picture. Anyways, he broke
our group's unsettled silence when he spoke:

"I see your bags are labeled 'ORD.'
While I'm a local driver normally,
I'll make exception for a modest fare.
My bus is small, but it'll get us there.
The roads are plowed and salted. It's no ploy.
Just follow me, we'll drive to Illinois."

The cons of traveling 'cross the state by bus
with Fred the Simpleton were obvious
and plentiful. But when I looked around —

observed the masses camped out on the ground,
monopolizing every inch of space—
my pious hesitation was replaced
with claustrophobia. I turned to Fred.
"You got yourself a deal. Let's go," I said.

The first in line, I waited to be seated
while Fred attended to my bag and greeted
me with a slight and sympathetic nod
and careful effort not to poke or prod
and/or, in any way, attempt to steer
my rotten attitude with words of cheer.
For misplaced glee would only stir the turd
of discontent. Fred didn't say a word.

The inside of the bus left much to be
desired. The seats were old and rickety.
The lights were dim and emanated gloom.
It smelled like deep-fried chicken and perfume.
I chose a spot in back and used the view
to scrutinize the others, like I do.

A dorky-looking lady with red hair—
and thick, black spectacles and skin so fair
her gangly veins popped out—sat right behind
Fred's seat. She said, "I wish these chairs reclined,"
and heaved a helpless sigh. She wore a fake
fur coat and matching boots. Give me a break.

The next one on the bus was just a wisp
of man. His hair was short, his tie was crisp.

He wore a blazer made of corduroy
and seemed to be too fucking full of joy.
He smiled at me, sat one row forward, and
he had a big-ass Bible in his hand.
So help me, if he tries to pros'lytize,
I thought, *I'll nail him right between the eyes.*

The third guy was a monster: tall and black
and built just like a Pro defensive back,
but, as it turned out, cloddy as could be.
He stumbled down the aisle awkwardly
and tripped a couple times before he chose
the seat across from Bible Man. Suppose
our sorry bus broke down, this hulk would be
the one to push us single-handedly —
until his clumsy legs gave out beneath
him and he fell and knocked out all his teeth.

The fourth, an old guy, sat across from Fake
Fur. He was French and thought it a mistake
that smoking on the bus was not allowed.
In fact, without his briar pipe, he vowed
to be "a crab for the entirety."
Thank God he sat up front and not by me.

The fifth and final misfit on this trip?
A woman, maybe twenty-five, equipped
with biker jacket, matching leather pants
and multiple tattoos. Her warning glance
at me conveyed, "Don't make me kick your ass."
She sat across from me, this dainty lass.

Fred wasted little time. He cranked the heat
and jotted something down and put his seat
belt on, then shut the door and sealed our fate;
we left the airport for the interstate.

As we began our trek through Michigan,
an agitated boredom settled in.
While making travel plans, not one of us
had factored in five hours on a bus.
We stared outside the window at the drear,
and Fred observed us in his rear-view mirror.
He cleared his throat and said, "Just thought I'd mention—"
and paused to try to beckon our attention.
Well, who else are we going to listen to?
I thought. The Bible Man replied, "Please do."

So Fred proceeded. "Anyone inclined
to telling tales?. . . .If so, then in your mind
create your finest story and relay
it to the rest of us. Of course, it may
be fact or fiction, any topic's game.
The story-teller who's the best will claim
a free ride on this bus. I'll reimburse
the winner for the merit of their verse."

We picked apart the offer Fred had made,
concerned with how each story got its grade.
"Majority decides," Fred said. "You'll cast
a single ballot following the last.
And to be sure that fairness will prevail,
you have to vote for someone else's tale."

A couple people feigned uncertainty
about the rules, but I think, secretly,
they did it to buy time so they could find
a story in their heads that would outshine
the competition. Fred piped up again,
"So, people, are you out or are you in?"
We had no better way to pass the hours,
so we agreed to test our verbal powers.
And, thus, with little time to tweak her verse,
the Fake Fur Lady offered to go first.

[2]

THE FAKE FUR LADY'S TALE

"**M**y tale," she said, "has fetishes, a dose
of magic, vulgar language, and a gross
misunderstanding. Will you be offended?"
Fred cautiously inquired, "Could you amend it
or maybe tell a different tale instead?"
The Biker Chick spoke up: "Just go ahead.
For freedom of expression is the whip
that keeps in line the beast of censorship."
Nobody argued, so the stage was set
for Fake Fur Lady's story of regret:

"Within a small town did a woman dwell.
Her name was Mary Beth—which fit her well,
for she was shy and floated like a fairy
all day at work inside the town's library.
She wore bright dresses and a ponytail
and loved to read: it made her feel unstale.
When time allowed, she'd lurk among the shelves
and watch the patrons reading to themselves.
Then, when the day was done, she spent her eves
attending to her garden, raking leaves,
and watering the flowers. She believed
in honoring the beauty nature weaved.

Now, odd as it may seem, her sex drive lacked.
Although she met her share of men, in fact,
considered handsome by society,
her passions weren't remotely stirred, so she
refused to date. Her second quirk was that
men tended towards large bosoms. Hers was flat.
She tried a push-up bra, which made things worse.
'Mosquito bites' were naturally her curse.
Her love life in a nutshell? Low on luck—
she had small breasts and didn't want to fuck.

Until one day, while scanning in a book,
she heard a noise and turned around to look.
She saw a handsome man with dark brown hair
and bright green eyes—and in a wheelchair.
When Mary Beth glanced down, what did she see?
His leg was missing just above the knee.
His shorts exposed a fully-healed stump,

the sight of which provoked her heart to jump—
not from disgust, as flaws like this invited—
but seeing it, her passions were ignited,
and instantly she wanted him in bed.
The spell was interrupted when he said,
'The book I wish to read is on a shelf
but placed too high to take it down myself.
Would you assist me with this simple task?'
'Of course, I will,' she said. 'So glad you asked.'
She kept him under lusty, close inspection
the whole way to the literary section.

He stopped and pointed: 'See that book in blue?'
She nodded, grabbed a stool, and said, 'I do!'
And as she reached up high to get the book,
he gave her silhouette a hearty look.
At once he held his breath, tried to stay cool.
In front of him were breasts so miniscule
and beautiful—and contoured perfectly,
'cause watermelons weren't his cup of tea,
but rather half a handful did the trick,
at least before his accident. How sick
he was of feeling constantly left out
because he couldn't stand or walk about.

And so he stole a final, fleeting glance.
Then she stepped down and broke him of his trance
and said, 'Here is your book, *The Works of Shelley*.
He is my favorite, so oblige to tell me:
familiar, are you, with Romantic style?'
'I am,' he said and flashed a little smile.

They spoke of Byron, Wordsworth, nature's pen
until they reached the checkout desk again.
She scanned his book and he glanced at her tit.
She caught him looking just a little bit.
And, likewise, when he reached to tie his shoe,
she eyed his sexy stump—he caught her too,
and said, 'My name is Henry, by the way.'
'And mine is Mary Beth. Enjoy your day.'

He left the building, headed to his van,
and Mary Beth, enamored by this man,
observed him drive away into the sun.
'Oh my,' she thought, 'could Henry be—The One?'
She organized some books into a bin
while in a daze and with a silly grin,
and when her supervisor came along,
he chastised her: 'You've rearranged these wrong!'
Poor Mary Beth said 'Sorry!' and turned red.
'There's no excuse. I'll fix it now,' she said
and labored hard to reinstill his trust.
Though sober, Mary Beth was drunk with lust.

And when at night she finally hit the hay,
her fantasies of Henry turned risqué.
She hugged her pillow, wishing it were him
in all his glory, with his missing limb,
and in her dreams she touched his crippled part
while kissing him. She woke up with a start
at dawn and panicked for she knew her bosom
was puny and she didn't want to lose him.
'What can I do,' she fretted in the mirror,

'with breasts so small they're barely even here?
I saw him glancing at them by the desk.
He's got to think my flat chest is grotesque.'
She eyed herself and thought with trepidation,
'If only I could get an augmentation.
My wage is modest though. My car is old.
I have no savings, jewelry or gold.
How would I finance such a costly plan
to change myself and thus seduce this man?'

She teetered on the brink of bleak despair,
then thought a way around it. Would she dare?

A single valued item she possessed
could yield the money to enlarge each breast.
She bolted through the bedroom to the back
far corner of her closet, moved a rack,
and knelt and pried the floorboard which revealed
a modest firebox, securely sealed.
She opened it and, wrapped in velvet, found
a copy of *Prometheus Unbound*.
A tattered book, it had been handled plenty,
a first edition, dated eighteen-twenty,
left to her in her Great Aunt Esther's will
some years before. She loved her great-aunt still—
for all the guidance and support she gave
to Mary Beth, who as a youngster craved
to learn about what other people thought.

As you can well imagine, she was fraught
with angst, for now her passion was reborn

to spend her life with someone. She was torn.
For should this most desired book be sold
so Mary Beth could fit a silly mold?
I think you know the answer, as do I,
but Mary Beth's decision went awry.
She wanted desperately to land the fish
and trumped her instincts with her anxious wish.

So carefully she wrapped the book up tight
and searched for book collectors who just might
be interested in this lengthy tome
and for a price provide it with a home,
so in return she'd get a hefty check
and drastically 'improve' her upper deck.

Now, Henry, when he left that sunny day,
said to himself, 'I need to find a way
to woo this Mary Beth, with breasts so fine,
and literary tastes, to make her mine!'
He thought about how beautiful she was
but quick became depressed and all because
his lack of limb preempted such a date,
or so he thought. He wallowed in self-hate:
'There's nothing I can do to make it fair.
This amputation is my cross to bear.'

But then a thought occurred to him at last,
a hopeful, dreadful way to change the past.
He knew of someone who communicated
with apparitions and facilitated
grim séances and magic that was black.

His name was Damon. He lived in a shack
beneath the beauty of this happy town
and lurked within its bowels, underground.
And Damon had a filthy, matted beard.
He never cut it, which was pretty weird.
'Just maybe,' Henry pondered, 'if I ask,
he'd carry out this most uncertain task.'
So Henry headed to his rusty van
and drove in search of Damon, Magic Man.

And on his way to find him, Henry passed
by Mary Beth, whose die had just been cast:
her book received a bid for seven grand,
and, just like that, she sold it. Check in hand,
she found a doctor who would change her cup
for seven thousand dollars. She signed up
and when she paid him, it was history:
she said good-bye to A, hello to D.

Now Henry parked his van and wheeled around
and headed towards the shanty. But the ground
was muddy. He got stuck and couldn't move
at all — as if the gods had disapproved
of Henry's plan and wanted to prevent
his ill decision. But he was intent
on changing his deformity. He tried
with all his might, and finally he pried
his wheelchair free and headed towards the shack,
which cast an eerie glow and aura black.
Then Damon stepped outside into the light.
His eyes were sunk, his skin was pasty white.

He watched his visitor suspiciously,
then scratched his beard and said, 'Please follow me,'
and led him inside which was candle lit.

Then, squinting, Henry said, 'I must admit
I've heard about your powers, so I beg
of you to implement them on my leg
and heal it properly, so once again
I'll have mobility like other men.'

And Damon nodded, and he said, 'I see.
However, what you ask is hardly free.
What do you have to offer in return?'

Poor Henry scoured his brain. He didn't earn
a dime to spare. He had no capital.
His only asset was intangible.
So finally he spoke with apprehension:
'The only thing I have is education.
I haven't watched TV in quite awhile,
for literary classics are my style.
I love to read and learn about the past.
My understanding of the world is vast.
That's all I have, I'm sorry there's not more.'

He backed away and headed towards the door.
But Damon said, 'Hang on a minute there,
'cause I can help you ditch your wheelchair.
For fifty years my magic's worn me out—
destroyed, beyond the shadow of a doubt,
my curiosity for learning stuff.

It sounds to me as though you have enough
intrinsic interest in the world we live.
So if, in fact, you're predisposed to give
this over to me, then I'll mix the brew
which magically will build your leg anew.'

What good is knowledge when you're all alone,
thought Henry. He decided to disown
his love affair with language and instead
pursue the one with Mary Beth. He said,
'Without mobility my love life's wrecked,
so go ahead and take my intellect.'

And Damon smiled and heated up his pot
and added liquids, herbs and lizard snot
and random parts of rodents and their piss.
He poured two glasses. Then he stated this:
'May demons act as witness to this pact.
Enhance my mind, and make his leg intact!'
They drank the potion down and lightning fell
and knocked them both unconscious for a spell.

They finally stirred; Black Magic Man was first.
He said, 'I think my brain has been immersed,
for I remember words I've never heard
and can recite the classics word for word!'

And Henry felt for where his stump would be.
There was a leg, and he sprang up with glee
and said, 'At last!' and ran back to his van.
He left his wheelchair with Magic Man.

As happy Henry was that afternoon,
the future, sadly, hummed a different tune.

When Mary Beth returned to work post-op,
attention from the fellas was nonstop.
They hit on her and tried to ask her out.
She thwarted their advances, for no doubt
their main attraction wasn't to her mind
but twenty inches down they were inclined
to stare. She tuned them out, for she had hope
that Henry would return and he would grope
her any way he pleased. And, likewise, she
would fondle his abrupt deformity.
Together they would relish all their days,
discuss Romantic authors and their ways
of seeing nature and imagination.
She fantasized about this conversation.
How blissfully complete it made her feel
to find, in Henry, someone who appealed
both to her brain and her libido too —
at least she thought, but it was far from true.

For moments later, as she pushed a cart,
she had her dream of Henry blown apart,
for in he strode without his wheelchair.
He stole behind her, smiled and said, 'Hey there!'
She craned her neck. 'What happened to…you know?'
The way she said it made him lose his glow.
'I thought…' he started, but he trailed off.
She veiled her disappointment with a cough
and said, 'So can I help you find a book?'

He hung his head in shame, for he mistook
his knowledge as disposable. He said,
'I'm sorry. I no longer am well-read.
It was the price I paid to walk again.'

He tried explaining further — that was when
she turned, he saw her breasts, and then he got
full-blown repulsed. They sickened him a lot.
I can't believe she did that, Henry thought.
And Mary Beth was equally distraught
'cause he forsook his assets, as it were.
His passion gone, he said good-bye to her.
And she to him, and Henry left that place
no longer yearning after second base,
for Mary Beth had massacred each boob.

So Henry bee-lined home, turned on the tube,
and watched a dozen hours a day or more
for years. Eventually he wed Victor-
ia, a most austere and joyless prude.

And Mary Beth combated all the rude
and raunchy comments when the guys would flirt
and try to cop a feel beneath her shirt.
And she developed problems in her back
from having such an ill-proportioned rack.

So, forced to give up gardening, she sat
alone at night, regretting mostly that
her insecurities had made her choose
to base herself on trite, external cues

instead of knowing in her heart that she
was just what nature wanted her to be.

So, each of you, be cautious. That's my plea,
for false assumptions breed conformity,
and in the race to fit the mold, you'll find
you've left your truest sense of self behind.
So *celebrate* your quirks — they'll set you free —
and raise your glass to authenticity."

[3]

THE BIBLE MAN'S TALE

The dingbat with the Bible offered to
go next. "Though you may have a different view,"
he said, "please grant me space to execute
religious freedom in this small pursuit."
It didn't sound like he was going to try
to cram his tenets down my throat, so I
allowed him room to carry out his whim —
which, oddly, was about a missing limb
as well, though only metaphorically.
So here's his tale, a Christian tragedy:

"There was a child named Calvin who was raised
within a church where 'God' was always praised,

and 'Jesus' too. The Bible was the key —
it spelled out right and wrong with certainty.

Young Calvin had short hair and was straight-laced,
and never entertained a thought in haste.
His favorite children's Bible story was
the one where Noah built the ark because
God told him to. For forty days they sailed
while all the wretched sinners screamed and wailed
and died. But Noah's boat was safe and sound,
till finally it stopped on solid ground.
The animals onboard were then released.
They ran and flew and swam away in peace.

Apparently, Jehovah felt regret
for drowning men because He was upset
about the evil in the world. He sent
a rainbow, his symbolic covenant.
He promised not to end the world with flood
(and later offered hope through Jesus' blood).

How Calvin longed to have a special 'ark'
where only light existed — nothing dark
or if it did, then righteous he would be
to squelch it and return to purity.
And to his flock, he'd spell out God's command
and lead them safely to the promised land.

Because he had charisma and was very
determined, Calvin entered seminary.
He studied both Creation and the Fall.

The Psalms, the Gospels — he absorbed it all
and read the Ten Commandments carefully,
and all the laws of Deuteronomy.
And thus with honors Calvin was ordained,
a Master's in Divinity obtained.

It wasn't too long after graduation
that he was called to serve a congregation.
His sermon voice was angry, which worked well,
especially at sparking fear of hell
and warning those who'd fallen from the path
that their repentance could reverse God's wrath.

As much as Calvin loved his job, his life
was missing something meaningful: a wife.
He took this great concern to God above
and prayed He'd bless him with a spouse to love.
Then, Sunday, as he read the scripture text,
foreshadowing the sermon that came next,
he glanced across the pews in search of those
whose minds had wandered off — and then he froze.
For Calvin spied a single woman who
was thin and beautiful — and Christian too!

So following the benediction he
made sure to greet each member casually.
And when he got to her, he shook her hand
and introduced himself. Her face was tanned,
her eyes were blue, her teeth were pearly white.
Her voice was reassuring and polite.
Rebecca was her name, as it turned out.

She seemed accommodating and devout.
'I'd like to spend some time with you,' he said.
They dated for awhile and soon were wed.

Within a year of marriage, Calvin and
Rebecca had a baby on their hands.
Her name was Hannah Joy, and she was blessed
with parents who had chosen righteousness,
for Calvin preached his hardest to ensure
his daughter's future world was just and pure.

One day, because his sermons were well-known,
a Christian station called him on the phone.
'We like your style,' he said. 'Please help our mission.
We'll feature you on cable television.'
And Calvin was delighted! He agreed!
A TV show would help his church succeed.
He'd reach more sinners, save them from the dark,
and thus expand his sacred, righteous ark.

So people tuned him in on Sunday mornings
to hear his sermons on the Bible's warnings.
'God's people,' Calvin said, 'You can't be friends
with God and sinners both, so make amends
by cutting off your sinful hand or arm
if doing it will keep your soul from harm.
And do not let the liquor touch your lip;
it is a sign that Satan has his grip
on you. And, likewise, if you choose to act
on wrongful inclinations, you'll attract
God's wrath. For sexuality was meant

to be enjoyed by man and wife. Repent
if you have ever entertained a lust
of someone who is not your spouse, and just
ask God to make your spirit right and pure.
And also, prostitutes are Satan's lure,
and films R-rated, and especially
the sin of homosexuality,
for God Himself so carefully defined
it as a sin that's of the deepest kind.

So if you find a sinner in your midst
who's unrepentant, please acknowledge this:
the message clearly comes from God above.
It's surely for the best to show tough love
and cast him out until he sees the light,
and has repented fully and is right
with God again. Preserve your sanctity
and cleanse the church from this impurity!'

And at the sermon's end, the congregation
rose up and gave a thundering ovation.
And Calvin smiled, for finally he felt
he'd made his niche within the Bible belt.
He swelled with pride for squelching sinful vermin.
However, he would soon regret that sermon.

For in a tiny house three states away,
a married couple watched TV that day
and listened to the sermon carefully.
They'd struggled for a decade privately
because they had a son named Thomas who

had evidently turned from what was true.
For as a youth he played with dolls instead
of trucks, and dressed in women's clothes and said
he hated football. So he spent his hours
redecorating and arranging flowers.
His senior year he finally made it clear.
He sat his parents down and said, 'I'm queer.'
And they were shaken up but let him stay
at home — until they heard the preacher say
that tough love was the Godly way to act.
And so they told him, 'Get your bags and pack!
For we no longer can condone your sin.
When you repent, you can return again.'

So, devastated, Thomas left his town
and wandered aimlessly until he found
a group of homeless guys who were replete
with street-smart ways to help him make ends meet.
He sold the morning paper, dug through trash,
donated plasma for a little cash,
and made a cardboard sign, in his despair,
that asked if strangers had some change to spare.

It gnawed upon poor Thomas' soul that he
was ostracized by his own family.
But he was headstrong. He had no intent
to acquiesce and forcefully repent.
His parents, though they claimed to be devout,
in his mind, had no right to kick him out.
For where does Man's will end and God's begin?
What sort of Savior labels love a 'sin'?

Still, homeless life weighed heavy on his chest,
and he became increasingly depressed.
The other homeless men took note of it
and tried to comfort him a little a bit
with words of kindness and encouragement.
But he was wounded to a great extent.

Now, as for Calvin, he continued to
enjoy his popularity, accrue
more followers to see the Bible's worth,
and bring about God's kingdom here on earth.
His greatest blessing, though, was easily
his daughter Hannah who was turning three.
So Calvin and his wife planned something great:
a birthday party — thus to celebrate!

In front of Hannah they set down the cake
and said, 'Blow out the candles and please make
a birthday wish!' She tried but couldn't gather
enough air in her lungs. And it was rather
discouraging for Calvin and his wife.

They blew them out themselves, and with a knife
divided up the cake, and gave a bite
to Birthday Girl, who had no appetite.
They tried to spoon it in to no avail.
Rebecca noticed, 'Doesn't she look pale?'
And Calvin nodded, not sure what to do.

A few days later, they decided to
admit her to the doctor, who ran tests,

while Calvin prayed that Hannah would be blessed
with health, and she would soon recuperate.

But sadly that was not his daughter's fate.
The doctor met with them and said, 'I've got
some bad news for you both. Your daughter's not
in tip-top shape because her blood's not right.
She's got leukemia.' And so in spite
of Calvin's faith, he had been dealt this blow.
How quickly happiness transformed to woe.
'What can we do about this situation?'
he asked. The doctor said, 'We need donation
of marrow from a person whose profile
will match your daughter's. It might take awhile.
We'll do the best we can to serve this case
by searching through the nation's database.'

The summer months wore on into the fall.
Then, long at last, they finally got The Call.
 'Our search turned up a possibility,'
the doctor said. 'In fact, most recently
the guy donated plasma. He's your match.
Convincing him to donate is the catch.'

So Calvin hopped a plane, his plan to say
the right things to this person and then pray
the guy would see the graveness of the issue
and willingly give up his crucial tissue.

When Calvin showed up at the said address,
with every good intention to impress,

he rang the bell. Who answered in plain view?
The married couple. They said, 'We know you!
You are the famous preacher from TV.'
And Calvin nodded, smiled, and said, 'That's me.
I'd like to speak with Thomas, if I may.'
The woman shook her head and said, 'He's gay.
Because he would not cling to what was true,
we kicked him out just like you told us to.'

'Where is he now?' asked Calvin frantically.
'We aren't too sure,' they said, 'but likely he
is living on the streets. We recommend
you find the river bank where homeless tend
to congregate. Just head four miles west.'
'I thank you both,' said Calvin, 'and God bless!'

He drove precisely where the couple said
and parked, continuing on foot instead.
He climbed the river bank and looked around
for Thomas, who was nowhere to be found.
He pulled a photo from his pocket, which
showed Thomas' face, and jumped into the ditch
where several men were sitting by a fire.
With vehemence he spelled out his desire.
The men replied, 'We know of whom you speak
but haven't seen him in at least a week.'

So Calvin climbed back out and searched the land,
which was deserted — save an older man
who stood along the bank and glanced into
the stream, as if deciding what to do.

So Calvin took a breath, accosted him.
He flashed the photo, and his voice was grim:
'I do request your knowledge, if I may.
I'm looking for a Thomas, who is gay.'

The old man studied Calvin. Then he said,
'I'm sorry, but the one you seek is dead.
For Thomas spiraled into great despair.'
He pointed. 'Do you see that bridge up there?
Last week your Thomas stood on it and leapt.
He was depressed. I tried to intercept
him, talk him out of it. I had no chance.
His soul was damaged by his circumstance.'

Hysterically, poor Calvin searched the water,
refusing to accept his dying daughter.
But with the current all his hopes were swept,
and Calvin crumbled to his knees and wept.

And when he got back home, he couldn't bear
to, once again, assume the pulpit there.
For had he kept his mouth shut, he derived,
his daughter's marrow match would be alive.
Instead poor Hannah waited hopelessly
for marrow that she simply wouldn't see.

It didn't matter how hard Calvin tried
to alter things. His precious daughter died.
They buried her in utter disbelief
and suffered such an overwhelming grief,
a sadness, and a loss of such great force

that Calvin and his wife sought a divorce.
Abandoned by his passion and his spunk,
there was no rainbow. Calvin's ark had sunk.

Amidst the grieving and forsaken bliss,
there is a lesson to be learned from this.
Before you amputate a 'sinful' arm
to save your precious church from Satan's harm,
you might embrace this underrated view:
what's done unto your 'least' is done to you."

And through the dark, our little bus forged forth—
Grand Rapids was directly to our north.

[4]

THE BIG CLOD'S TALE

The clumsy fellow stretched and bumped his head.
"Those stories ended tragically!" he said.
"I'll tell mine next, if you're inclined to hear it.
Things turn out well, so it'll lift your spirit.
However, though I'm black and also male,
I'll mention this disclaimer to my tale:
one character's a woman and she's white,
and while I don't pretend to know the plight
of those outside my gender or my race,
nevertheless, I hope you will embrace
the notion that it's possible to choose

to picture life in someone else's shoes.
I need creative license for this plan."
"Sure. What the hell," we said. The guy began.

"There was a young man, full of attitude.
He grew up in the hood and so the dude
feared none. This brother had more courage than
a foxhole soldier in Afghanistan.
When he was five, he watched his father die
and two years later nearly lost an eye.
His name was Sammy, and he had a scar
across his cheek from fighting in a bar,
and had a bullet buried in his chest.
At six foot four and bald, you didn't mess
with Sammy. As a bouncer, his vocation
demanded backbone and intimidation.
His job was to protect the nightclub, so
he weeded out the gangstas like a pro.

It's fair to say that Sammy would exude
a recklessness endowed with fortitude,
because he liked his liquor, I won't lie,
and smoked his blunts and always had his eye
on women who were fine. Uncharted land
would often turn into a one-night stand.
He liked this woman Desiree, but she
would not put up with promiscuity.
He asked her out. She flatly told him, 'No.
You've got to recognize I'm not a ho.'
But Sammy's impulse was so deep-engrained
he'd no idea how to act restrained.

One afternoon he planned on getting high
while on his way to work, but his supply
of Zig-Zags had run out so, needing more,
he made a stop at the convenience store.

He stood in line and noticed, to his right,
a woman who was affluent and white.
I bet that woman's got an easy life,
thought Sammy. *Bet she never has no strife.*

What went down next was crazy and bizarre.
The woman turned to him and said, 'You are
inaccurate. My life has much distress.
Perhaps you shouldn't try to second-guess
my circumstance. Your thoughts are quite untrue.'
And, flabbergasted, Sammy said, 'How do
you know what I am thinking?' And without
replying with her voice, she freaked him out.
I do not know, she thought, and Sammy heard
her plain as if she'd spoken every word!
Then she continued on, *You think I've got
it easy in this world but I do not.*
I bet my life is harder. Sammy scoffed.
Like hell it is, he thought. It pissed him off
to think she'd be so bold as to suggest
her silver spoon would trump his Bullet Chest.
Then something even crazier transpired;
believe me, it was neither one's desire.
The line moved forward and their elbows bumped —
that single action caused their souls to jump
into each other's bodies. Suddenly

poor Sammy wasn't who he used to be.
Instead his hair was blonde, his skin was white,
and he wore heels. He mumbled, 'This ain't right.'
And just the same, the woman was amazed,
for she felt tall and strong and when she gazed
upon herself, her skin was dark. She said,
'How did this happen?' Then she stepped ahead
and bought the papers Sammy'd come there for
and in his body promptly left the store.

And Sammy, strangely stricken with this curse,
paid for his gas with money from his purse.
He also left the store, assumed the lady's
persona, and drove off in her Mercedes.

When he arrived at home, it wasn't at
his crib but hers, and *damn*, the place was phat!
He parked, unlocked the front door with the key,
and stepped inside the house. What did he see?
A bombass living room with leather chairs
and sofas, and a flight of spiraled stairs,
a plasma TV that was large and flat,
and pricey art. For sure, this habitat
was fine! He climbed the staircase to explore
extravagances on the second floor:
a king-size bed which had a canopy,
a bathroom with a marble vanity
and other rooms that seemed to be for guests.
They hosted feather beds and cedar chests.
Back on the main floor Sammy found, at last,
a modern kitchen — bright and clean and vast.

Placed on the countertop there was a note —
apparently a list the woman wrote
of all the errands that she had to do.
'Get gas.' He crossed it off. And next? 'Make stew
for dinner.' So he tenderized the meat
and found he knew exactly how to treat
the gravy to effect a tasty flavor
by adding certain spices. This behavior
wasn't Sammy's. It was left behind
by her, when their two lives were intertwined.
So Sammy used her skill and cooked with ease,
and said aloud, 'This woman's life's a breeze!'

The woman, all the while, drove Sammy's car.
Instinctively, she parked outside a bar.
She found beneath her seat a bag of pot,
but, knowing she was at her job, would not
consider smoking it. So she clocked in
as Sammy — with some newfound discipline.

She stood outside the club all night, I.D.ed
the patrons, and her presence guaranteed
a peaceful night. Some thugs were packing heat.
The woman grabbed them, tossed them on the street.
I'm strong as hell, she thought, *and not afraid!*
And when the women looking to get laid
approached her, she refused their bold advances —
excused herself from all such circumstances.

Back at the mansion, Sammy's gourmet meal
turned out to have a spicy, bold appeal.

The woman's husband came home after work —
and proved to be a narcissistic jerk.
He poured himself a scotch, and with a scowl
he plopped down at the table. 'This smells foul,'
he said. He shoveled in a bite, then said,
'I hate this fucking spicy food! You're dead!'
He rose and belted Sammy in the face,
and said, 'You sorry bitch. You're a disgrace.'

Now Sammy's eye swelled up from the attack.
He wanted nothing more than to fight back,
but in the woman's body he was weak
compared to this abusive psycho-freak.

So he retreated up the stairs to bed
and prayed the guy would stay away. Instead,
he heard the husband's footsteps drawing near,
so Sammy grabbed the comforter in fear,
and shouted, 'Please don't hit me anymore!'

The husband said, 'But that's what wives are for.
You better learn your lesson, understand?
'Cause when I say I like my meals bland,
I mean it.' Then the husband left the room,
and Sammy's soul was overcome with doom,
for he had never been this filled with fright
in all his life. *Perhaps the woman's right,*
he thought. *Her life is harder than I guessed.*
But that's no reason to remain oppressed.
She's crazy-disciplined with all her lists
but has no guts to discontinue this!

I think by using bravery I can
escape this trap. So he devised a plan.

Back at the club, the woman closed the bar
and locked it up and lumbered to her car.
She had enough of Sammy's memory
to figure out the route instinctively
and entered his apartment, where she shed
his shoes and jeans, and zonked out on the bed.

Now normally the bouncer would sleep in,
but in this case the woman's discipline
prevented it, so she was up by eight.
She noticed right away the filthy state
of his apartment, so she intervened.
From head to toe and front to back she cleaned
She vacuumed, dusted, mopped, and threw away
a ton of rotten food. It's fair to say
this was the cleanest Sammy's place had been
in seven years — since Sammy first moved in.
She opened up the closet in the hall.
What greeted her? A bright orange basketball.
She moved aside a cap and baseball mitt,
cleared out a bunch of other random shit.

But then she stumbled on the thing that could
transform the pothead bouncer's world for good.
It was a blues guitar in mint condition.
The woman picked it up, played a rendition
of Muddy Waters' classic song, 'Champagne
and Reefer' — borrowed from the bouncer's brain —

for she herself did not know anything
about the blues or how to pluck a string.
She strangely knew the words and sang along.
Her voice was deep, emotional and strong.

When she was done, she thought reflectively,
The black guy's got some talent, doesn't he?
So why's he working as a bouncer when
his musical abilities transcend –
she heard somebody knocking at the door.

She answered it and, greeting her, were four
young men who said, 'Hey Sammy!' and came in.
The first guy busted out a fifth of gin.
The second guy whipped out a bag of chronic.
The third? A single blunt of hydroponic.
The fourth guy had a pint of Hennessey.
Their mission at his place? No mystery.
They poured the liquor into plastic cups
and rolled the chronic, and they fired up
the hydro, but before they caught their buzz,
the woman said, 'You gotta leave because
you caught me in the middle of a chore.
I need more time.' She pointed towards the door.
'That's cold!' the homies said. 'Since when ya' choose
your precious "chore" instead of weed and booze?'
'Since now. I am not kidding!' she announced.
And so the homies grabbed their shit and bounced.

Alone, she pondered Sammy's discontent
and contemplated his predicament.

He lives impulsively, she thought, *and tends*
to buckle under pressure from his friends.
Although he's fearless, he is caught within
a trap. I'll free his mind with discipline.

She hunted for a music teacher who
was focused on basics and was true
to the creative processes. She signed
on for some lessons and was disinclined
to kick it with her friends. Instead, for hours
a day she worked to hone her music powers.
She paid her bills by bouncing at the bar,
but every day she practiced that guitar.

Now in the meantime, Sammy thought he would
appease his asshole husband best he could.
(For all the turmoil Sammy underwent,
at least the husband turned out impotent.)
So he was careful that the meals he made
were void of spices, so they'd make the grade
and give the fucker one less reason to
erupt into a rage and come unglued.
So Sammy bode his time and played the part
and learned that eggshell-walking was an art.

Now, luckily, the guy worked twelve-hour days,
and Sammy mustered up a grip of ways
to spend his free time—which he didn't waste.
He found a health club and he joined in haste
and wrote a list and set up a routine—
employing an elliptical machine,

a stationary bike and running track
and free weights. After that he would attack
the punching bag till he was near collapse,
then hit the pool and swim a dozen laps.
He signed up for a class in self-defense
and drank a bunch of protein supplements.

He worked out in the mornings. Then, at noon,
he quit and showered. In the afternoon
he practiced cooking meals with devices
like crockpots, steamers, skillets. He used spices
abundantly and tested out each dish
of chicken, lamb chops, sirloin steak, or fish;
and conjured up creative recipes
with vegetables like squash or baby peas.

He tasted every meal and refined
the flavor with an aptly chosen wine.
He wrote down all the recipes that proved
to be exceptional. And then he moved
each tasty dinner that he had perfected
directly to the garbage, undetected,
and cooked up something uninspired and bland
to pacify his husband's lame demand.

Because he spent his mornings working out
and afternoons on culinary bouts,
he didn't spend a dime on fancy clothes
or haircuts or the painting of his toes
or jewelry. Instead he chose to stash
into a hiding place the excess cash.

For months this was the way he operated —
until the evening he initiated
a massive change. He made a bland dish for
his husband just like every day. Before
he cooked it, though, he failed to clean the pot,
so spices lingered that were super-hot
from earlier when he made peppered veal.

The husband took a big bite of his meal
and spit it out and stated loud and rude,
'I cannot eat this fucking spicy food!'
Enraged, the guy rose up and tried to hit
his wife. But Sammy ducked and said, 'This shit
is over!' All those hours of exercise
paid off. He punched him hard between the eyes.
The husband staggered back and dropped his scotch,
and Sammy up and kicked him in the crotch.
The guy fell to the floor and gasped, 'This stunt
will get you nowhere fast, you filthy cunt!'
'You're wrong,' said Sammy. 'You will not harass
me anymore! I'm gonna dump your ass!'

He bolted to his secret hiding place
and stuffed his money in a pillowcase.
He grabbed his keys and headed towards the door.
Then, glaring at his husband on the floor,
he said, 'I'm outta here. This marriage blows,'
and kicked him one more time — and broke his nose.

The next day Sammy found a place to stay,
a small apartment twenty miles away.

He hired a lawyer, filed for a divorce,
and fought for half of everything. Of course,
he got it, too — a million and a half,
along with something else: the final laugh.
He used the money to fulfill a want —
her strong desire to own a restaurant.
He bought a vacant building, overhauled
the dining area, and then installed
necessities like ovens, freezers, sinks,
and stocked the place with tasty food and drinks.
He planned to be there for the great event:
Grand Opening! But that's not how it went.

For on that day, filled with anticipation,
he stopped at a familiar destination:
a small convenience store to purchase gas.
He stood in line to pay and then — at last —
he heard a voice behind him. 'You are me!'

He turned and saw the man he used to be —
the fearless bouncer. Sammy said, 'You're right!
And I am you — still just as blonde and white.
It's nice to meet again,' he said and shook
his former body's hand. But all it took
was that one touch — the pair of souls switched back,
and she was white again, and Sammy black.
'I am myself!' said Sammy. 'And you're you!
I think we have some catching up to do.
I dumped your husband, now you live alone —
without abuse. You're strong and fit, and own
a restaurant that's opening tonight!'

The woman instantly expressed delight.
'I've always wanted one! How did you do
it?' Sammy said, 'With discipline that you
already had. Plus I replaced your fright
with bravery.' The woman said, 'All right,
I need to tell you how you've changed your ways.
No longer do you have that stoner glaze
or sleep with skanks. You now have discipline
to complement your courage. You have been
developing your musical career.
You play the blues. Tonight is your premiere.'

'That's been my dream!' said Sammy. 'Thanks a lot!'
He tried to hug her. She said, 'Better not.
Don't want to switch again.' And he agreed.

'Good luck to you,' he said. She said, 'Indeed,
the same to you.' And then they parted ways
to live their dreams for their remaining days.

Because she'd been uprooted from duress,
the woman's restaurant proved a great success.
She served her patrons with a newfound pride
and flavors she no longer had to hide.

And Sammy went that night and played his set,
with melodies that no one would forget.
And afterwards, he heard a voice say, 'Hey!'
It was that classy lady, Desiree.
She complimented him and they exchanged
kind words, for she could tell that he had changed

and had a more selective attitude.
A meaningful relationship ensued.

Now smaller venues with their curtain calls
turned into record deals and concert halls.
So this is how a bouncer-dude became,
in just a few short years, a household name.

The moral of the story's pretty clear,
that discipline alone disguises fear.
But courage on its own is just as lame —
a random shotgun blast without an aim.
Still, one provides commitment to a task,
the other gives us strength to even ask.
Together they afford the tools to build
a life that is successful and fulfilled."

[5]

THE FRENCH GUY'S TALE

The French Guy shifted in his seat and said,
"May we inject an intermission, Fred,
since smoking is forbidden on the bus?"
—a rule that didn't faze the rest of us.

Fred exited in Benton Harbor, where
we stopped at a convenience center there.
I used the restroom, stretched my legs, and bought
a snack. (In line to pay, I curbed my thought
and made sure not to inadvertently
bump elbows with the guy in front of me.)

When Jacque was finished with his nicotine,
we wrapped our pit-stop up and reconvened,
got settled, and resumed our late-night ride.
Jacque's attitude was freshly pacified.
He said, "My story has no violence,
abuse, or tragedy — just common sense."
We reassured him that it was okay.
He said, "Then I will speak now, *s'il vous plait.*

"There was an ancient university
that sat upon a hill prestigiously.
The lawn was green, the buildings made of brick.
So formal was the campus rhetoric
that pupils and professors both were prone
to speaking in an academic tone,
employing lengthy words pretentiously.

Within the college of philosophy,
there was a timeless fixture, so to speak,
a pedagogue who specialized in Greek.
His hair was silver, he wore wire-rimmed glasses,
and rarely taught the lower-level classes.
His own opinions grew to be quite firm.

Now, this professor chanced to have, one term,
three students who were hyper-motivated.
They sat in front, took notes, and instigated
disputes that sounded bitter and unkind,
for each was sure he had the brightest mind.

These three were so competitive that they
were not content to each have earned an A.
The old professor had the wherewithal
to stunt this cutthroat, academic brawl.
'I'll give a prompt,' he said. 'You'll have a week
to formulate your answers. Then you'll speak
for ninety seconds. He who answers best
will prove that he's the winner of this test.
I'll honor he who reigns victorious,
for to his "A" I will attach a "plus."'

He took the chalk and scribbled on the board
the words upon which hinged this great reward:
Which form of love is the most powerful?

The students instantly began to mull
the question over, analyzing ways
to tackle it in merely seven days.
'I'll offer up a hint,' said the professor,
concerned they'd veer off track on this endeavor.
'Romantic love's one possibility,
as is platonic camaraderie.
The final option is God's love for man.
You are dismissed. Now do the best you can.'

The three young rivals gathered up their books
while bickering and casting dirty looks.
They headed off in different directions
to flesh their thoughts out, further their reflections,

and, using evidence, try to persuade
their teacher they deserved the highest grade.

The week went by and everyone returned,
anticipating sharing what they learned.
They sat in front and each of them was dressed
in business suits. They wanted to impress
the pedagogue, who beckoned, 'Who goes first?'

The closest student stood and dove headfirst
into his argument. 'Romantic love,'
he said, 'has clearly set itself above
the rest. Its power cannot be dismissed:
without it neither you nor I exist.
Biology is why we copulate.
Our hormones are so powerful and great,
no other form of love could e'er defeat
the love which happens underneath the sheet.

Moreover, men have written poetry
and ballads long before this century.
In fact, you can look back at Song of Songs;
the Bible makes the case. This love's so strong
it has a February holiday
named after it. And just the other day,
I witnessed many couples on a date,
They emanated such a mental state
of pure euphoria. This love, it reigns!
It alters chemicals in people's brains.

In fact, romantic love contains the life
which prompts a man to court his future wife.
One gentleman I spoke to said he sold
his boat to buy a ring of solid gold
and multi-karat diamonds so that he
would dazzle and impress his wife-to-be.
So tell me, what could possibly exceed
romantic love in sentiment or deed?'
He gathered up his notes and took a seat.

The second student didn't miss a beat.
He cleared his throat and said, 'I have observed
a certain habit, whereby neighbors serve
each other every day. They monitor
the neighborhood for thugs. If they're not sure
as to exact intentions of a stranger,
they question him, and if they sense a danger,
they will escort him from the neighborhood —
a preservation of the common good.

Moreover, when a neighbor needs a hand
to fix a roof or execute a plan
to renovate a bathroom or a den,
his loyal buddies hustle over. Then,
on weekend afternoons, they congregate
at someone's house to drink and to await
the kickoff of their favorite football team.
They *yea* and *boo*, high-five and yell and scream
and seal the bond. No love could e'er compare

to camaraderie that people share.'
He sat. The third guy stood and said, 'The love
that reigns most powerfully hails from above.
For I attended, just last Sunday morn,
a worship service meant for those reborn.
The church itself was intricate and vast
and reminiscent of traditions past.
The members of the congregation dressed,
without exception, in their Sunday best.
They listened to the sermon heedfully,
for it explained about eternity:
If you accept that Jesus died to save
you from your sins (and then rose from the grave),
you'd thankfully avoid your hellish fate
and God would let you past the pearly gate.

The solemn congregation then stood up
to take a drink from the communion cup
and eat a piece of bread. It signified
the flesh and blood of Jesus when he died.
They put their money in the offering plate
because their love of Jesus was so great.
They sang a hymn so loudly you could tell
that each was grateful he avoided hell.
In short, this proves a power not outdone:
God's love for us when we accept His Son.'

He sat. All three were sure that they would win.
Before the old professor could begin

to set the academic record straight at last,
there was a scuffling from the back of class.
Appearing was a woman who was dressed
in faded jeans and t-shirt. She expressed
a pressing interest in the task at hand.
'Although,' she said, 'it wasn't what you planned,
I'd like to share my view, if that's okay.'
The startled pedagogue said, 'Speak away.'

The three competing students scowled at her
and sighed with irritation. They were sure,
because her current grade was just a 'C,'
that they outshined her philosophically.
Unlike the three, she didn't read her part.
Instead she spoke impromptu from the heart.

'I listened carefully to this debate,
and while I do not wish to aggravate
the situation, I'm suggesting this:
a point is missed in each analysis.

Romantic love should win, allegedly,
because it's rooted in biology?
This argument is built on the reliance
that there's no bigger influence than science.
What's more, it was suggested love is gauged
by jewelry one gets when they're engaged.
Now, at the risk of sounding impolite,
these reasons for romantic love seem trite.

Platonic friendship claims it takes the cake
because the comrades willfully partake
in helping out, but there's a stipulation:
the understanding of reciprocation.
A common football team provides a bond?
How *that* could win this contest is beyond
me. Finally, in order to receive
God's love for us, we're prompted to believe
He sent His Son. But this is based on fear
of punishment. If we do not adhere
to it, then we'll be damned eternally?
That seems to miss the point of love to me.

Now, on *my* little quest to understand
the purest love, I asked three people. And
the first man had been married fifty years.
He said, "Romance is not what it appears.
You see, my wife's been ill. I've taken care
of her and held her hand through great despair.
I've bathed her, and I've wiped away her tears
and changed her diaper every day for years."

The second was a woman walking by.
"Well, normally I drive," she said, "but I
don't have a vehicle. There's been a streak
of burglaries along my street. Last week,
somebody stole my car and lost control
and smashed it straight into a metal pole.
The thief was fifteen and illiterate,

so our community chose to commit
to teaching him to read. Until his trial,
he's being held inside the juvenile
detention center, so we volunteer
to see him daily, and we try to steer
his interests towards the knowledge he can gain
from reading books, which cultivate his brain."

The third guy was a preacher. "I'll attack
that question. So you know, I just got back,"
he said, "from witnessing a hurricane
disaster. Mass destruction put a strain
on dozens of communities who were
quite destitute to start with. We made sure
they had a place to stay and food to eat
until the reconstruction was complete."
"Did you convert the people so they would
not go to hell?" I asked. He said, "What good
are promises of future's pearly gates
to people in the midst of dire straits?"

A diaper changed, a thug who learns to read,
and swift disaster aid to those in need —
the strongest love is that which will avow
to end the hell that men are living now.'

She sat back down. The pedagogue assumed
the floor, and there was silence in the room.
'I've pondered and assessed your arguments,'

he said, 'and each displayed intelligence.
However, one has earned the victory.
I have determined that, with certainty,
the man who went to church has won this test.'
In honesty, he liked his shoes the best.
Besides, the woman's 'heartfelt' speech destroyed
established categories. It annoyed
him greatly that she tried to spurn tradition
(*and* end a sentence with a preposition).
These blatant flaws proved that a woman's mind
was naturally restricted and confined — "

The Biker interjected, "What the hell!
This story's FUBAR! Women can excel
in academics just as well as men!"

"Perhaps," the French Guy said, "but then again
the story's mine, not yours. Accordingly,
I ask a little common courtesy."
The Biker frowned but put a lid on it.
"I will continue now, since you permit,"
he said. "And so the student swelled with pride
and got the perfect grade — and a full ride
the next year, so he didn't have to pay
a dime to carry on with his cliché.
Eventually he earned a Ph.D.
and a professorship where he was free
to let his classroom content represent
his loyalty to the establishment.

The woman's answer caused her grade to slip,
however, so she lost her scholarship.
Tuition cost too much so she dropped out.
She got a job assisting those without
a home to find a place to stay. She steered
away from empty words — and volunteered
at hospitals and women's shelters too.
And so her life experience proved true
to her intent: to build community
and spread compassion exponentially.

And so my story ends. Perhaps you've learned
that trusting institutions gets you burned.
Or schools reward the docile, not the smart.
Or maybe you should listen to your heart.
But pack *this* in your pipe and smoke it through:
the question-asker regulates the view.
Consider, then, this possibility:
that life's an essay, not a choice of three."

And on that note, we entered Indiana.

THE BIKER CHICK'S TALE

The Biker Chick adjusted her bandana
and dropped her voice all low, like her vocation
could be a DJ on a hard rock station.
"This story's true," she said, "and I admit
the character goes through some awful shit."
So here's the story by the Biker Chick,
delivered in uncensored rhetoric:

"There was a little girl named Phoenix. She
came from a super-fucked up family.
Her dad got drunk, her mom did drugs, and then
things often escalated. Sometimes when

the fighting got too loud, she'd try to get
reception on her bedroom TV set.
Because they lived out in the boondocks, though,
the only channel — 4 — would come and go
depending on the weather. So she took
the family's battered VCR and hooked
it to her crappy TV. She would play
the only film she owned — about a stray
but smart and friendly dog. Her favorite scene
was when he saved these little kids from mean
adults who kidnapped them. So she rewound
that part and played it over with the sound
cranked up to drown her yelling parents out.
Each time she watched the movie, without doubt,
it spurred a dream in her that someday she
would own a dog who'd love her faithfully.

In spite of all the hope that film bestowed,
it didn't change the facts. Her parents owed
the neighbor for a gram of low-grade tar
and, just like that, they pawned the VCR.

Then, when the girl was ten, her mother ran
off with a cocaine dealer. So the plan
was for her dad to raise her. But he was
abusive, and he beat her just because
he felt like it. He used his leather belt
and hit her with the buckle end. Each welt
bled hard and turned into an ugly bruise.

And once, after he drank a fifth of booze,
he struck her with a wooden baseball bat
and broke her leg. She told the doctor that
she'd fallen from a tree — 'cause she surmised
her dad would get in trouble otherwise.

When they removed the cast, it was revealed
her leg was bent unnaturally. It healed
all whack. So Phoenix wore long pants to school
to try to thwart the schoolyard ridicule.
It didn't work. She still walked with a limp,
and, cruelly, students nicknamed her 'The Gimp.'

Then, shortly after starting puberty,
she hit rock-bottom, for her dad could see
she was maturing. So he made her wear
a ton of makeup and no underwear.
Then all his friends came over and got lit,
and he encouraged each of them to hit
on her. Against her will, she filled their need.
Suffice to say they made the poor girl bleed.

In high school, Phoenix drew the wrong attention
from just the kind of boys whose ill intentions
would further strip her of integrity.
So, sure enough, she put out easily
and had a reputation as a slut.
At times she tried to change her habits, but
her sucky self-esteem meant she was trapped.

Then, late one night, her father *really* snapped.
An iron pipe in hand, he tried to hit
her with it. He was drunk and high as shit.
She ran but wasn't fast enough. Instead,
he knocked her out. She woke up in the shed,
a brittle, wooden building. When she tried
to leave, she couldn't. She was locked inside.

The shed was almost empty; there was not
a single item left except a cot.
She heard her father's footsteps drawing near.
He opened up the door and reeked like beer
and stated, 'This will be your place to stay.
I told the school that you have run away.'
He forced her on the cot and roughly used
her just the way he wanted. The abused
girl tolerated this for thirty days,
till she was liberated by a blaze.

For on that night, her father showed up for
his drunken, vulgar visit. As he bore
down hard upon her, she astutely slipped
her hand into his jacket pocket, gripped
a box of matches he had left in there.
When he was finished, he took extra care
to make sure that the door was locked. She waited
until she thought he was intoxicated
enough to pass out in his favorite chair,
so then he'd be completely unaware

of what was happening. The time seemed right.
She struck a match. It cast a hopeful light,
and carefully she held it to the shed
along its driest side. The fire spread
reluctantly at first — but then it grew.
She stripped the linens from her bed and threw
the metal cot frame through the burning wall.
She swallowed hard and then prepared to crawl
out through the opening. But excess smoke
filled up the room. Her eyes burned and she choked.

As if to ascertain her father's wrath,
a burning ember fell and blocked her path.
However, she resolved to persevere;
her long for freedom overcame her fear.
So, coughing, she endured the smoke and spark,
dove through the flames, and landed in the dark.

She snuck into the house. The clock struck one.
She listened hard for voices — there were none.
She spied her dad passed out just as predicted,
and hated him for all he had inflicted
upon her, but she didn't dwell on it.

She grabbed some clothes and cash before she split,
then shut the door behind her, hurried down
the road. She stopped, and one last time glanced 'round.
Was fate, or just coincidence perhaps:
she watched the shed — engulfed in flames — collapse.

An hour later, nursing but a grain
of hope, she found the tracks and jumped a train.
For two days straight she traveled on this way
until she reached an ample place to stay.
It was a massive city where she could
get lost in crowds and shake her past for good.

She left the train and found a greasy spoon,
and while she ate she figured she would soon
be out of money, so she'd need a source
of income. But she had no skills, of course,
except to disassociate her thoughts
whenever acting sexually. She fought
against it mentally because that route
just wasn't what her 'new life' was about.
She knew, however, she could make a buck
in lightning speed by charging men to fuck.
And so she found the seedy district quick
and, temporarily, planned to turn a trick.

She stood out on the street until a guy
inside a car slowed down as he drove by.
He stopped and rolled the window down and said,
'How much ya' charge to give a little head?'
She wasn't sure how much to say because
she'd never done a thing like this. She was
naïve in her own way. And so she took
a guess and said, 'Uh, thirty bucks.' He looked
her up and down, unlocked the door, and said,

'Climb in.' His confident approval fed
her hopes of cash. They drove three blocks away
and parked in a deserted alleyway.

Then he unzipped his pants. She did the deed,
and thankfully he came in record speed.

When it was time to pay, he flat refused.
But Phoenix wouldn't let it go. 'Excuse
me, where's my pay?' she asked. But he denied
he owed her. 'Get the fuck outta my ride,'
he said. She sat there stubbornly. The guy
at once flew off the handle — grabbed her by
the hair and yanked her out onto the street.
He punched and kicked repeatedly — he beat
her hard. She doubled over. Then he smashed
her in the face and left her by the trash
cans lined along the concrete wall. He fled
the alley in his car, left her for dead.

A distant thunder rumbled with disdain.
She spent the night unconscious in the rain.

But in the morning — after daylight broke —
a most peculiar stimulus provoked
the girl back into consciousness.
It was a moist sensation, so she guessed
it to be drizzle, but it wouldn't quit.
She raised her head, sat up a little bit,

It wasn't dripping rain, she realized.
It was. . .a licking tongue? Aptly surprised,
she opened up her eyes to what affair?
A dirty, beaten dog just standing there.
His ears were cropped, his legs were scraped and cut,
his hip and rib bones were protruding, but
he still looked muscular. He had a chain
embedded in his neck. She ascertained
that if this scarred-up, brindle pit could tell,
he'd certainly disclose the private hell
he had been living. But he couldn't speak.
Instead he simply stood and licked her cheek.

Since getting beaten up was not her plan —
her clothes were caked with blood, her makeup ran —
she had to get cleaned up and reconsider
accepting rides from strangers. They might hit her
just like the motherfucker from the night
before. She found a warehouse, out of sight,
and brushed her hair, changed clothes and reapplied
her makeup. When she reappeared outside,
the dog was waiting. 'Get away!" she said.
'I mean it!' He just followed her instead.

She stowed her backpack filled with extra clothes
behind a dumpster. Then she recomposed
herself, preparing for a second chance
to turn a trick and hopefully finance
some food to live on and a place to stay.

A car pulled up, but to the girl's dismay,
the dog came from behind the dumpster and
growled low and deeply at the horny man
inside the car. The guy said, 'Fuck it,' when
he saw the dog, and left the scene. And then
the girl got pissed and shooed the dog away.
'You can't do that!' she said. He wouldn't stay
away from her, however, so she tied
him to the dumpster, out of sight. He cried
and whined while she attempted to solicit—
her efforts were cut short by an explicit
and most exacerbating scraping sound.
She stopped what she was doing, turned around.
The dog, who had refused to be confined,
had labored towards her. And what dragged behind?
The iron dumpster she had tied him to!

She squatted down and started reprimanding
him but stopped short. She saw an understanding—
deep in his eyes—she'd never seen before,
a knowingness that struck her to the core.
There was no senseless bullshit or abuse
or wooden sheds or assholes to seduce—
just blind compassion streaming from his soul.
His presence seemed to naturally console
her pain. Then, from the sidewalk, someone yelled,
'Is that your dog?' The girl glanced up. Compelled
to claim him after all, she nodded yes.
'He sure is strong,' the guy said. 'Let me guess.

Are you the one who taught the dog to pull
the dumpster all that way?' There was a lull.
Then Phoenix said, 'Okay, about that, when—'
'Impressive!' and he gave the girl a ten.
The girl looked at the money in her hand
then at the dog who seemed to understand.
He wagged his tail and did a little dance
as if to say, *This happened not by chance*
but forces that you do not know exist.

Excitedly, the girl bent down and kissed
the dog. And then—inspired to act—she laid
an empty hat upon the ground and made
a sign. It read, 'Amazing Dog! No lie!'

And people on their bikes or driving by
or walking down the sidewalk stopped to see
the canine move the dumpster. Luckily,
the folks were so impressed and dazzled that
the girl discovered money in her hat.
And some guy took a video of it,
uploading it onto the internet.

So in the evening, from her makeshift bed
inside the empty warehouse, Phoenix fed
three hot dogs to the famished dog, ate three
herself. She pet the canine tenderly
and said, 'Your name is Buddy and I'll keep
you always.' And she got a great night's sleep.

When they arrived next morning at their spot,
the pair of people greeting them was not
what they expected. Dressed in business suits,
they said, 'We're agents scouting for recruits
and saw you on the web, just so you know.
We'd like to have you on our TV show.'
Then Phoenix looked at Buddy: 'Whatcha think?'
He wagged his tail and with a single blink
conveyed to Phoenix stoic fearlessness.
She turned back to the scouts and said, 'Hell, yes.'

And just like that they both were whisked away
by limousine with minimal delay
and taken to a hotel where they stayed
for free because the program's budget paid
for it. The next day they went to the set
where each contestant gathered with their pet.

The atmosphere was crazy and intense —
spurred by a live and rowdy audience.
Then, one by one, each pet trick came and went
till it was time for Buddy's grand event.

She harnessed Buddy to the dumpster and
made eye contact, so he would understand.
Then Phoenix gave the go-ahead. He plowed
successfully across the stage. The crowd
erupted in applause! He was a smash!
They scored first place and won a ton of cash!

Exposure from the pet-themed TV show
inspired a children's film producer. So
he pitched a storyline to Phoenix: when
a stray dog meets a lonely youngster, then
they form a friendship, end up fighting crime
and rush to be there in the nick of time!

Well, Phoenix loved the story. She agreed
to feature Buddy in it, and indeed,
the film became a hit. With seeming ease,
she started raking in the royalties.
She bought a spacious home with grassy ground
where Buddy had the space to run around.
She got a motorcycle and attached
a sidecar with a custom-fitted hatch.
Because they both adored the open road,
they oftentimes were gone from their abode.

Was well past dark one night when they arrived
to a familiar truck parked in the drive.
It was her father's. On the porch he stood.

'Long time, no see,' he said. 'Perhaps we could
get caught up, don't you think?' And then her dad,
intuitively sensing that he had
the upper hand, took but a single stride
in her direction. She was petrified.
Her courage faltered, but her dog's did not,
and in a flash he bolted 'cross the lot

and chased the asshole once around the truck
into the bed. He shouted, 'What the fuck!'
'Caught up yet?' she responded. Then she called
her dog off, and her father quickly crawled
into the cab and peeled away like mad.
That was the last time Phoenix saw her dad.

The years wore on, and two more films were made
where Buddy cultivated his crusade
against injustice. She was more than set
financially, but she could not forget
her life experience. She never wed
for she had too much baggage. She instead
ensured what went around came back around
by volunteering at the local pound,
and fostering the dogs who faced demise —
and were at risk for being euthanized.

Upon the final film's release, it was
announced that Buddy would retire because,
said Phoenix, he deserved to sleep past dawn
and spend his hours basking on the lawn
instead of being taught a new routine
just so the cameraman could film the scene.

Although his muzzle had begun to gray,
he still had years left, and he loved to play
with Phoenix and the other dogs. He'd run
and keep up even with the youngest one.

One evening when the sun began to set —
a crimson sky and tree-lined silhouette —
and Phoenix sat relaxing on her deck,
she realized that she forgot to check
the mail. So with Buddy close behind,
she went out to the box. What did she find?
A single, plain white envelope without
a trace of where it came from, and made out
to Buddy. Curious, she walked back to
the house, opened the note and read it through.

Dear Buddy, said the letter. *I adore*
you, and I want to tell you thank you for
your movies, cuz I watch them every night.
You see, my parents always scream and fight.
To drown them out, I play your DVD.
I'm only ten years old but, hopefully,
someday I'll own a dog as cool as you.
The note was signed, 'Sincerely, Betty Lou.'
And Phoenix held the letter close and prayed
and, hugging Buddy, watched the sunset fade.

Just like my tale, the moral's also true
though it may sound implausible to you.
Dream loudly and the universe will hear,
and someday what you dreamt of may appear."

7

THE NARRATOR'S TALE

Conclusion of the biker's tale meant
I was the only one left to present.
Before I had the option to begin,
the driver Fred looked up and he jumped in:
"We're exiting the freeway, so we'll be
arriving at the airport rapidly.
Still, if you can, you're more than welcome to
relay a shortened version, so that you
will have a chance at winning back your fare."

To tell the truth, I didn't think that there
was any way I could abridge my tale

without omitting relevant detail.
I could start telling it till time ran out
and forced me to abandon it, no doubt,
like others through the centuries had done,
deserting midway through what they'd begun.

Nevertheless, the present's not the past:
I didn't want my tale to sound half-assed.
"Because I wish to finish what I start,"
I said, "I will refrain from taking part.
I think the rest of you should vote instead
to see which one gets reimbursed from Fred."

The other people said that wasn't fair
to me. I shrugged and said, "Somehow, somewhere,
although it wasn't able to unfold
tonight, I sense my story will be told
eventually. And that will have to do.
It's lengthy, and the minutes left are few."

Reluctantly, the others acquiesced
and shifted focus to which tale was best.

8

THE WINNER

And so at last the time had come to score
the tales. The Fake Fur Lady voted for
the one about the students who were trite,
the Big Clod found the one with Phoenix tight.
The Biker Chick enjoyed the story that
involved the woman's bosom that was flat.
The tale the Bible Man chose to embrace
was when the bouncer and the blonde switched place.
The storyline that topped the French Guy's list
portrayed the rigid televangelist.
So, thus, the voting outcome went awry,
for it resulted in a five-way tie.

The storytellers simply weren't content
with such results, and so an argument
ensued. Before it got too out of hand,
the driver Fred said, "I can understand
the conflict here, so I propose that we
resolve it fairly." Then he glanced at me.
"You are the most objective person here.
Would you oblige us all and volunteer
to cast a vote, determining the verse
that's best, so I'll know who to reimburse?"

I nodded yes, and all eyes quickly turned
to me. Each storyteller was concerned
that I would treat them fairly, and I would,
but first I messed with them — because I could.
"The Frenchman triumphs," I announced in jest,
"because — why else? — I like his shoes the best."

The other storytellers gave me hell,
objecting adamantly till I yelled,
"I'm kidding!" Then they simmered down. "Okay,"
I said, "I think it should go down this way.
It's clear that, by your ballots, you agree
that each tale has its merit. I decree,
therefore, in fairness, Fred should keep the dough
because he got us where we wished to go
and made the time pass quickly with this game.
By listening to these stories we became
distracted, and what started out distraught
transformed into a ton of food for thought —
a literary appetizer for

the bounty that tomorrow has in store.
So Fred's earned every penny of this trip.
Moreover, I encourage you to tip
him generously as you disembark.
His journey home is solo in the dark."

I paused to let them picture Fred forlorn,
a lonely traveler on Thanksgiving morn,
and realize that what I said was true.

It turned out to be timely spoken too.
For Fred pressed forward to the terminal—
a blast of diesel fumes and windshield full
of brake lights—and adeptly found the place
reserved for busses, slipped into a space
proficiently and with the utmost care,
and stated brightly, "Welcome to O'Hare."

9

THE GENERAL EPILOGUE

We waited on the curb. Fred handed us
our luggage, which he'd stowed upon the bus
five hours before. We thanked him verbally
and backed our words up monetarily.
For in addition to some dough, Fred scored
fresh jerky made from venison, a horde
of snacks from Benton Harbor, plus a gift
bag, fruitcakes, homemade jelly, and a fifth
of high-end bourbon. "Thanks," he said. "Good-bye."
And then the bus let out a little sigh.
"I guess it's time to hit the road again.

I've got my family back in Michigan."
He closed the door and pulled away into
the flow of traffic. Disappeared from view.

Then those of us remaining said farewell
and happy holidays. We heard a yell,
and Fake Fur Lady ran and climbed inside
a rusty, old-school van, which was her ride.

The Bible Man waved "Bye!" and jumped into
a rainbow-stickered BMW.

The Big Clod saw a classy woman near
the temporary lot. "I'm over here!"
he shouted — and he stumbled on the curb.

The French Guy smoked his pipe and looked disturbed
until he spotted, in the pickup lane,
a gray sedan. He waved it down and strained
to see inside. It must have been the right
one. He jumped in and slipped into the night.

As for the Biker Chick, she'd come to see
her grandmother who was apparently
residing in a nursing home and was
the only next of kin she had because
her parents "sucked." She wished me well and went
inside to find a vehicle to rent.
And for the first time — since I left the plane —
I noticed that the Biker used a cane.

Her exit left me standing all alone,
adjacent to the fresh-plowed loading zone,
which sparked a thought about this whole event.
When blizzards bury us in discontent
and strand us in a drift of misery,
our shovel is our creativity,
and each new path we dig reminds us that
we're more than just another stupid rat.

The moment was abruptly interrup-
ted when a yellow taxicab pulled up.
With gratitude and nothing to retract,
I grabbed my bag and climbed into the back.
The end had come, and so I shed the rhyme
and shut the door and vanished into time.

ACKNOWLEDGMENTS

Thanks to my family and friends for their ongoing encouragement and support, with a specific shout-out to my brother Bill, who I can always count on to "feed the frenzy."

Thanks to Linda Fox, Harvey Stanbrough, and the various folks who have given me feedback in writing classes and poetry groups.

And a special thanks to Joanne Vigilant for believing in my writing all along.

**CATHY SPROUL** was born and raised in south suburban Chicago. She holds a B.A. in Communications and English from Calvin College (Grand Rapids, Michigan) and an M.A. in Creative Writing/Satire from Prescott College (Arizona). Her prior works have appeared in *Teacher Magazine* and *The Door*. A high school English and mathematics teacher, she currently lives in Tucson, Arizona, where she works with at-risk youth, promotes responsible dog ownership, and creates bad puns.